John Brown, Clementina Stirling Graham

Mystifications

John Brown, Clementina Stirling Graham

Mystifications

ISBN/EAN: 9783337419080

Printed in Europe, USA, Canada, Australia, Japan

Cover: Foto ©Andreas Hilbeck / pixelio.de

More available books at **www.hansebooks.com**

MYSTIFICATIONS

By CLEMENTINA STIRLING GRAHAM.

Fourth Edition.

Health to the auld wife, and weel mat she be,
That busks her fause rock wi' the lint o' the lie,
Whirling her spindle and twisting the twine,
Wynds aye the richt pirn into the richt line.

EDINBURGH:

EDMONSTON AND DOUGLAS.

1869.

Contents.

Contents.

THESE delightful *Mystifications*, which were privately printed four years ago, have been so much sought after in this country and in America, that I have prevailed—not without difficulty—on Miss Graham to let the public, as well as her friends, enjoy them.

" Those who knew the best of Edinburgh society eight-and-thirty years ago—and when was there ever a better than that best?—must remember the personations of an old Scottish gentlewoman by Miss Stirling Graham, one of which, when Lord Jeffrey was victimized, was famous enough to find its way into *Blackwood*, but in an incorrect form."

" Miss Graham's friends have for years urged her to print for them her notes of

these pleasant records of the harmless and
heart-easing mirth of bygone times ; to
this she has at last assented, and the
result is this entertaining, curious, and
beautiful little quarto, in which her friends
will recognise the strong understanding
and goodness, the wit and invention, the
fine humour of the much-loved and warm-
hearted representative of Viscount Dundee
—the terrible Clavers.[1] They will recall
that blithe and winning face, sagacious

[1] "DEAR DR. BROWN,—In compliance with your re-
quest, I send you my genealogy in connexion with
Claverhouse—the same who was killed at Killie-
crankie. John Graham of Claverhouse married the
Honourable Jean Cochrane, daughter of William Lord
Cochrane, eldest son of the first Earl of Dundonald.
Their only son, an infant, died December 1689. David
Graham, his brother, fought at Killiecrankie, and was
outlawed in 1690—died without issue—when the re-
presentation of the family devolved on his cousin,
David Graham of Duntrune. Alexander Graham of
Duntrune died, 1782; and on the demise of his last
surviving son, Alexander, in 1804, the property was
inherited equally by his four surviving sisters, Anne,
Amelia, Clementina, and Alison. Amelia was my
mother.

"Yours ever,

"CLEM. STIRLING GRAHAM.

"DUNTRUNE, 14th November 1860."

and sincere, that kindly, cheery voice, that rich and quiet laugh, that mingled sense and sensibility, which met, and still, to our happiness, meet in her, who, with all her gifts and keen perception of the odd, and power of embodying it, never gratified her consciousness of these powers, or ever played

> ' Her quips and cranks and wanton wiles '

so as to give pain to any human being.

"And are we not all the better for this pleasantry? so womanly, so genial, so rich, and so without a sting,—such a true diversion, with none of the sin of effort or of mere cleverness; it takes us into the midst of the strong-brained and strong-hearted men and women of that time; what an atmosphere of sense, good-breeding, and *couthiness!* And then the Scotch! blossoming out everywhere as blithe, expressive, and unexpected as a gowan or sweet-briar rose. Besides the deeper and general interest of these *Mystifications*, in their giving, as far as I know, unique specimens of true personation—distinct from acting—I think it a national good to let our youngsters read, and, as it were, hear the language which our Scottish gentry and judges and men of letters spoke not long ago, that language in which what is best of Robert Burns may —if we cease to know and use it—ere long lie buried. Was there ever anything so good said of a stiff clay, as that it 'girns (grins) a' simmer, and greets (weeps) a' winter'?"[1]

When we read over the names we find here, we see the men, we hear them, and feel their living power. There is Lord Newton, huge in body and in mind, capable of any mental and social effort, full of hard reason. William Clerk, only less witty and odd than his great Swiftian brother, Lord Eldin. Lord Rutherfurd, then young, but rejoicing, as only a strong man does, to run his race, with those great, burning, commanding eyes, and that noble head. Lord Gillies, every inch a man and a judge—strong, clear, prompt, inevitable, with a tenderness and concentration of heart that only such men

[1] *Horæ Subsecivæ*, Second Series, 1861, p. 328.

can have and give. I remember well his keen, shrewd, handsome, authoritative face, his shapely, well-knit legs in his Hessian boots.

- There is Harry, afterwards Lord Cockburn, with those wonderful eyes, melancholy and lonely, brown, clear, and deep as a muirland tarn, sparkling at times as if an unseen sun shone on them, or oftener as if a star of their own twinkled from out their depths; but their habitual expression pensive to melancholy: what nature and fun and pathos! what a voice, what homely power! and his long country stride and his black gaiters, as of a country minister—his leisurely flow of soul, rippling but strong, singing a quiet tune to himself, and turning everything to his humour,— as native, as inimitable, as unmade and exquisite as a roadside flower or spring.[1]

[1] It would be endless to give instances of his peculiar humour. It was mild in tone, and didn't explode so much as expand; but for quiet and intense exaggeration I don't know anything to equal it. We all remember his "Edinburgh is as quiet as the grave, or even Peebles." One day, coming down the Mound from Court, about five P.M., a friend met him, and said, "You're looking tired: have you been all this time in

And there is Jeffrey, whom flattery, success, and himself cannot spoil, or taint that sweet, generous nature—keen, instant, unsparing and true as a rapier; the most painstaking and honest-working of all clever men; such eyes! and that mouth, made to speak to and bewitch women— mobile and firm, arch and kind, with a beautiful procacity or petulance about it, that you would not like absent in him, or present in any one else. Michael Angelo Taylor, the conjunction of whose names is glory and peculiarity enough. John Archibald Murray, handsome, courtly, bountiful; strong and full of courage when put to it, and on occasion not to be trifled with. Count Flahault, bright, gallant, and *galant*, proud of his English, prouder of his whist. It is said that when in Edinburgh about this time, the Count having beaten a famous whist-player, and being asked by him with *quasi* nonchalance and *à propos* of his having been one

Court?" "Yes," he said querulously; "it was that man ——." "Did he take up your time at that rate?" "Time! he exhausted Time, and encroached on Eternity."

of Napoleon's aides-de-camp, " How did Bonaparte look after the battle of Waterloo ?" replied, " Just as you do, sir."

And moving about, the greatest and naturallest of them all, like a Newfoundland dog or his own Maida among his fellows, Sir Walter, the healthiest and manliest of our men of letters—frank, open, and full of work as the day; with that homely, burly frame, that shrewd, *pawky* face, with its grey eyes and heavy eyebrows, its tall, tower-like skull (he used to say his hat *was* small, but then he filled it !)—eyes, when at rest heavy, filled with latent genius and story, " like music slumbering on its instrument;" when awake and lighted from within, how alive, how full of fun, making his rich voice and rich laugh all the richer ! He was then at his zenith ; he was after that to go down in that lamentable fight— fighting as few men ever did against such odds—ruined as such a man could only be, by himself;—by his own romantic, fatal weaknesses and strengths; we have no nobler piece of virtue in the old

Greek sense of manliness, than in his
leading on alone his forlorn hope, sticking to his colours to the last, and giving
in only when the brain, his weapon,
gave way and failed. I remember him
about that time: he used to walk up
and down Princes Street, as we boys were
coming from the High School, generally
with some friend, and every now and then
he stopped, and resting his lame leg
against his stick, laughed right out at
some joke of his friend's or his own : he
said a good laugh was worth standing for,
and besides required it for its completion.
How we rejoiced when we took off our
bonnets, to get a smile and a nod from
him, thinking him as great as Julius Cæsar
or Philopœmen, Hector or Agricola, any
day. I can fancy I see and hear him as
he bends down to "Mrs. Arbuthnott of
Balwylie," and says, with his rich *burr*
rolling in his mouth, and in her ear—
"Awa! awa! the deil's ower *grit* wi'
you."[1]

[1] The following account of Scott's impressions of this
performance is taken from one of his Journals :—

And the women of these times, how worthy—how, in scientific phrase, complementary of the men!—meeting them in all common interests half way, neither more nor less,—their companions, well read, well bred, free yet refined, full of spirit and sense—with a strong organ of adhesiveness, as our friends the phreno-

" *March* 7.—Went to my Lord Gillies's to dinner, and witnessed a singular exhibition of personification. Miss Stirling Graham, a lady of the family from which Clavers was descended, looks like thirty years old, and has a face of the Scottish cast, with good expression, in point of good sense and good humour. Her conversation, so far as I have had the advantage of hearing it, is shrewd and sensible, but no ways brilliant. She dined with us, went off as to the play, and returned in the character of an old Scottish lady. Her dress and behaviour were admirable, and the conversation unique. I was in the secret, of course, did my best to keep up the ball, but she cut me out of all feather. The prosing account she gave of her son the antiquary, who found an auld wig in a slate quarry, was extremely ludicrous, and she puzzled the Professor of Agriculture with a merciless account of the succession of the crops in the parks around her old mansion-house. No person to whom the secret was not intrusted had the least guess of an impostor, except one shrewd young lady present, who observed the hand narrowly, and saw it was plumper than the age of the lady seemed to warrant. This lady, and Miss Bell of Coldstream, have this gift of personification to a much greater degree than any person I ever saw."

logists would say. I wish we had more, or many, of such women now-a-days : women who, with all their gifts and graces, were always womanly in their ways and speech, and as distinct in character, each from the other, as were the men—or as is a beech from a birch, a lily from a rose.

Four worthies—one of them fourfooted —have been added ; the reader will wish there had been more. *Miss Menie Trotter*, like *Meg Matthew*, is an exquisite *study*, as the painters say, for a story. As you let-your mind rest upon it, you feel it unfolding itself into a life.

J. B.

23 RUTLAND STREET,
March 8, 1865.

TO MISS CARNEGY,

OF LAVEROCK BANK HOUSE.

MY DEAR FRIEND,

"THE MYSTIFICATIONS" are now going to make their début in the " wide wide world," and there is no one so well qualified, or with so good a right, to introduce them as the HEIRESS OF PITLYAL, the dear ROSEBUD herself.

There are few survivors of those pleasant evenings ; your beloved sister, Mrs. Gillies, and many more of the bright spirits have passed away, but they live again in the breathings of the past, and may yet give a spark of life to a weary hour.

Ever your affectionate,

CLEM. STIRLING GRAHAM.

DUNTRUNE, 1865.

b

ORIGINAL DEDICATION.

DUNTRUNE, *April* 1859.

MY DEAREST MRS. GILLIES,

To you and the friends who have partaken in these " Mystifications," I dedicate this little volume, trusting that, after a silence of forty years, its echoes may awaken many agreeable memorials of a society that has nearly passed away.

I have been asked if I had no remorse in ridiculing singularities of character, or practising deceptions ;—certainly not.

There was no personal ridicule or mimicry of any living creature, but merely the personation or type of a bygone class, that had survived the fashion of its day.

It was altogether a fanciful existence, developing itself according to circumstances, or for the amusement of a select party, among whom the announcement of a stranger lady, an original, led to no suspicion of deception. No one ever took offence: indeed it generally elicited the finest individual traits of sympathy in the minds of the dupes, especially in the case of Mr. Jeffrey, whose sweet-tempered kindly nature manifested itself throughout the whole of the tiresome interview with the law-loving Lady Pitlyal.

No one enjoyed her eccentricities more than he did, or more readily devised the arrangement of a similar scene for the amusement of our common friends.

The cleverest people were the easiest mystified, and when once the deception took place, it mattered not how arrant the nonsense or how exaggerated the costume. Indeed, children and dogs were the only detectives.

I often felt so identified with the character, so charmed with the pleasure manifested by my audience, that it became painful to lay aside the veil, and descend again into the humdrum realities of my own self.

These personations never lost me a friend; on the contrary, they originated friendships that cease only with life.

The Lady Pitlyal's course is run; she bequeathes to you these reminiscences of beloved friends and pleasant meetings.

And that the blessing of God may descend on " each and all of you," is the fervent prayer of her kinswoman and executrix,

CLEMENTINA STIRLING GRAHAM.

AT the theatre one Saturday evening in the year 1821, Mr. Jeffrey—afterwards Lord Jeffrey—requested me to let him see my *old lady*, and on condition that we should have some one to *take in*, I promised to introduce her to him very soon. Accordingly, on the Monday having ascertained that he was to dine at home, I set out from Lord Gillies's in a coach, accompanied by Miss Helen Carnegy of Craigo as my daughter, and we stopped at Mr. Jeffrey's door in George Street between five and six o'clock. It was a winter evening; and on the question, "Is Mr. Jeffrey at home?" being answered in the affirmative, the two ladies stepped out, and were ushered into the little parlour where he received his visitors.

There was a blazing fire, and wax-

A

lights on the table ; he had laid down his book, and seemed to be in the act of joining the ladies in the drawing-room before dinner.

The Lady Pitlyal was announced, and he stepped forward a few paces to receive her.

She was a sedate-looking little woman, of an inquisitive law-loving countenance ; a mouth in which not a vestige of a tooth was to be seen,[1] and a pair of old-fashioned spectacles on her nose, that rather obscured a pair of eyes that had not altogether lost their lustre, and that gave to the voice as much of the nasal sound as indicated the age of its possessor to be some years between her grand climacteric and fourscore. She was dressed in an Irish poplin of silver grey, a white Cashmere shawl, a mob cap with a band of thin muslin that fastened it below the chin, and a small black silk bonnet that shaded her eyes from any glare of light.

Her right hand was supported by an

[1] This fraud she accomplished by drawing her lips over her own natural set of good white teeth.

antique gold-headed cane, and she leant with the other on the arm of her daughter.

Miss Ogilvy might be somewhere on the wrong side of twenty; how many months or years is of no particular importance. Her figure, of the middle size, was robed in a dress of pale blue, and short enough in the skirt to display a very handsome pair of feet and ankles. On her head she wore a white capote, and behind a transparent curtain of pure white blonde glanced two eyes of darkest hazel, while ringlets of bright auburn harmonized with the bloom of the rose that glowed upon her cheeks. Her appearance was *recherché*, and would have been perfectly *lady-like*, but for an attempt at style,—a mistake which young ladies from the country are very apt to fall into on their first arrival in the metropolis. Mr. Jeffrey bowed, and handed the old lady to a comfortable *chaise longue* on one side of the fire, and sat himself down opposite to her on the other. But in his desire to accommodate the old lady, and in his anxiety to be informed of the purport of the visit, he forgot what was due to the young one, and the heiress of the ancient House of Pitlyal was left standing in the middle of the floor.

She helped herself to a chair, however, and sat down beside her mother. She had been educated in somewhat of the severity of the old school, and during the whole of the consultation she neither spoke nor moved a single muscle of her countenance.

"*Well!*" said Mr. Jeffrey as he looked at the old lady, in expectation that she would open the subject that had procured him the honour of the visit.

"Weel," replied her Ladyship, "I am come to tak' a word o' the law frae you.

"My husband, the late Ogilvy of Pit-lyal, among other property which he left to me, was a house and a yard at the town-end of Kirriemuir, also a kiln and a malt-barn.

"The kiln and the barn were rented by a man they ca'd John Playfair, and John Playfair subset them to anither man they ca'd Willy Cruickshank, and

Willy Cruickshank purchased a cargo of damaged lint, and ye widna hinder Willy to dry the lint upon the kiln, and the lint took low and kindled the cupples, and the slates flew aff, and a' the flooring was brunt to the ground, and naething left standin' but the bare wa's.

"Now it wasna insured, and I want to ken wha's to pay the damage, for John Playfair says he has naething *ado wi*' *it*, and Willy Cruickshank says he has naething *to do it wi*', and I am determined no' to take it aff their hand the way it is."

"Has it been in any of the Courts?"

"Ou ay, it has been in the Shirra-Court of Forfar, and Shirra Duff was a gude man, and he kent me, and would ha' gien 't in my favour, but that clattering creature Jamie L'Amy cam' in, and he gae it against me."

"I have no doubt Mr. L'Amy would give a very fair decision."

"It wasna a fair decision when he gae it against me."

"That is what many people think in your circumstances."

" The minister of Blairgowrie is but a fule body, and advised me no to gae to the law."

" I think he gave you a very sensible advice."

" It was onything but that; and mind, if you dinna gie 't in my favour, I'll no be sair pleased."

Mr. Jeffrey smiled, and said he would not promise to do that, and then inquired if she had any papers.

" Ou ay, I have a great bundle of papers, and I'll come back at any hour you please to appoint, and bring them wi' me."

" It will not be necessary for you to return yourself; you can send them to me."

" And wha would you recommend to me for an agent in the business ?"

" That I cannot tell; it is not my province to recommend an agent."

" Then how will Robert Smith of Balharry do ?"

" Very well; very good man indeed; and you may bid him send me the papers."

Meantime her Ladyship drew from her pocket a large old-fashioned leather pocket-book with silver clasps, out of which she presented him a letter directed to himself. He did not look into it, but threw it carelessly on the table. She now offered him a pinch of snuff from a massive gold box, and then selected another folded paper from the pocket-book, which she presented to him, saying, " Here is a prophecy that I would like you to look at and explain to me."

He begged to be excused, saying, " I believe your Ladyship will find me more skilled in the *law* than the *prophets.*"

She entreated him to look at it; and on glancing his eyes over it, he remarked, " that from the words *Tory* and *Whig,* it did not seem to be a very ancient prophecy."

" May be," replied her Ladyship; " but it has been long in our family. I copied these lines out of a muckle book, entitled the ' Prophecie of Pitlyal,' just before I came to you, in order to have your opinion on some of the obscure passages of it. And you will do me a great favour if you will read it out loud, and I will tell you what I think of it as you go on."

Here, then, with a smile at the oddity of the request, and a mixture of impatience in his manner, he read the following lines, while she interrupted him occasionally to remark upon their meaning :—

Extract from the Prophecie of Pitlyal.

When the crown and the head shall disgrace ane
    anither,
And the Bishops on the Bench shall gae a' wrang
    thegither;
        When Tory or Whig,
        Fills the judge's wig;
        When the Lint o' the Miln
        Shall reek on the kiln;
        O'er the Light of the North,
        When the Glamour breaks forth,
        And its wild-fire so red
        With the daylight is spread;
When woman shrinks not from the ordeal of tryal,
There is triumph and fame to the house of Pitlyal.

[The Light of the North was Mr. Jeffrey—the Glamour was herself; but we must give the Lady Pitlyal's own interpretation, as she appeared unconscious of the true meaning.]

"We ha'e seen the crown and the head," she said, "disgrace ane anither no very lang syne, and ye may judge whether the Bishops gaed right or wrang on that occasion; and the *Tory* and *Whig* may no be very ancient, and yet never be the less true. Then there is the Lint o' the Miln,—we have witnessed that come to pass; but what the *Light of the North* can mean, and the *Glamour*, I canna mak' out. The twa hindmost lines seem to me to point at Queen Caroline; and if it had pleased God to spare my son, I might have guessed he would have made a figure on her trial, and have brought 'Triumph and fame to the house of Pitlyal.' I begin, however, to think that the prophecie may be fulfilled in the person of my daughter, for which reason I have brought her to Edinburgh to see and get a gude match for her."

Here Mr. Jeffrey put on a smile, half serious, half quizzical, and said—

"I suppose it would not be necessary for the gentleman to change his name."

"It would be weel worth his while, sir;

she has a very gude estate, and she's a
very bonny lassie, and she's equally related baith to Airlie and Strathmore;
and a' body in our part of the warld ca's
her the ' Rosebud of Pitlyal.' "

Mr. Jeffrey smiled as his eyes met the
glance of the beautiful flower that was so
happily placed before him; but the Rosebud herself returned no sign of intelli-
gence.

A pause in the conversation now ensued, which was interrupted by her Ladyship asking Mr. Jeffrey to tell her where
she could procure a set of *fause teeth*.

" *Of what?*" said he, with an expression of astonishment, while the whole
frame of the young lady shook with some
internal emotion.

"A set of fause teeth," she repeated;
and was again echoed by the interroga-
tion, " *What?*"

A third time she asked the question,
and in a more audible key; when he replied, with a kind of suppressed laugh,
" There is Mr. Nasmyth, north corner of
St. Andrew Square, a very good dentist;

and there is Mr. Hutchins, corner of Hanover and George Street."

She requested he would give her their names on a slip of paper. He rose and walked to the table, wrote down both the directions, which he folded and presented to her.

She now rose to take leave. The bell was rung, and when the servant entered, his master desired him to see if the Lady Pitlyal's carriage was at the door.

He returned to tell there was no carriage waiting, on which her Ladyship remarked, "This comes of *fore-hand payments*—they make *hint-hand wark*. I gae a hackney-coachman twa shillings to bring me here, and he's awa' without me."

There was not a coach within sight, and another had to be sent for from a distant stand of coaches. It was by this time past the hour of dinner, and there seemed no hope of being rid of his visitors.

Her Ladyship said she was in no hurry, as they had had tea, and were going to the play, and hoped he would accompany them. He said he had not yet had his dinner.

" What is the play to-night ?" said she.

" It is the *Heart of Midlothian* again, I believe."

They then talked of the merits of the actors, and she took occasion to tell him that she patronized the *Edinburgh Review.*

" We read your buke, sir !"

" I am certainly very much obliged to you."

Still no carriage was heard. Another silence ensued, until it bethought her Ladyship to amuse him with the politics of the country.

" We brunt the King's effigy at Blairgowrie."

" That was bold," he replied.

" And a pair of dainty muckle horns we gae him."

" Not very complimentary to the Queen, I should think."

Here the coach was announced, and by the help of her daughter's arm and her gold-headed cane, she began to move, complaining loudly of a *corny tae.* She was with difficulty got into the coach. The Rosebud stepped lightly after her.

. The door was closed, and the order given to drive to Gibb's Hotel, whence they hastened with all speed to Lord Gillies's, where the party waited dinner for them, and hailed the fulfilment of the "Prophecie of Pitlyal."

Mr. Jeffrey, in the meantime, impatient for his dinner, joined the ladies in the drawing-room.

"What in the world has detained you?" said Mrs. Jeffrey.

"One of the most tiresome and oddest old women I ever met with. I thought never to have got rid of her;" and beginning to relate some of the conversation that had taken place, it flashed upon him at once that he had been *taken in.*

He ran down stairs for the letter, hoping it would throw some light upon the subject, but it was only a blank sheet of paper, containing a fee of three guineas.

They amused themselves with the relation; but it was not until the day after that he found out from his valued friend Mrs. George Russell who the ladies really were. He laughed heartily, and promised to aid them in any other scene they liked to devise, and he returned the fee with the following letter :—

LETTER FROM MR. JEFFREY TO THE LADY PITLYAL RETURNING THE FEE OF THREE GUINEAS.

" DEAR MADAM,—As I understand that the lawsuit about the Malt-Kiln is likely to be settled out of Court, I must be permitted to return the fee by which you were pleased to engage my services for that interesting discussion ; and hope I shall not be quoted along with the hackney-coachman in proof of the danger of *fore-hand payments*. I hope the dentists have not disgraced my recommendation, and that Miss Ogilvy is likely to fulfil the prophecy, and bring glory and fame to the house of Pitlyal ; though I am not a little mortified at having been allowed to see so little of that amiable young lady.

" With best wishes for the speedy cure of your corns, I have the honour to be, dear Madam, your very faithful and obedient servant,

F. JEFFREY.

" 92 GEORGE STREET,
21st *April* 1821."

IT was arranged that there should be an evening party at Mrs. Russell's in honour of the Lady Pitlyal, before the wildfire should have time to spread, in order to give the benefit of an introduction to a few more of the Whig friends. The soiree was accordingly fixed for the Wednesday. We dined at John Clerk's (Lord Eldin's), where were several members of the supper party; and Mr. William Clerk took occasion to inform Miss Dalzell that the lady opposite had a talent for personating character. Mrs. Gillies and I took our departure soon after nine, as we had to stop in York Place to arrange the toilette of the Lady Pitlyal. Her Ladyship's dress this evening was abundantly conspicuous, and in the fashion of forty or fifty years back. It consisted of a gown of rich ponceau satin, open in

front, and drawn up like the festoon of a
window-curtain behind; a long and taper
waist, black satin petticoat embroidered
with roses of chenille, a muslin apron
trimmed with lace, a black lace Teresa,
and a stomacher fastened in front with
diamond rosettes, a point cap and a green
shade, with a veil, and spectacles to pro-
tect her eyes; on her feet a pair of embroidered shoes with high heels and large
silver buckles.

Miss Helen Carnegy declined personating the heiress any longer, so it was
agreed that the Rosebud should be engaged to a ball at our friend Mr. Baron
Clerk's.

We were announced and welcomed by
Mrs. Russell, and very soon the Lady
Pitlyal became the lion of the evening.
Ladies and gentlemen crowded round her.
Mr. Jeffrey made his bow, and entered
into conversation about the law plea, and
expressed disappointment at not having
the pleasure of meeting Miss Ogilvy.

Mrs. Simpson of Ogil alluded to their
estates being contiguous, spoke of her

family, and promised to bring them all to pay a visit at Pitlyal. Lord Gillies was reminded of the time when he was an *ill prettie laddie*, and of breaking the *lozens* of one of her windows, and Mr. Pillans inquired about the state of the roads. Mr. Russell asked if Prince Charles skulked about Pitlyal ? " Ou ay," she replied, " he span wi' the lasses." [1] He wondered if George the Fourth span with the lasses ? As to that she didna ken, but she thought he had managed to spin a ravelled hasp till himsel'.

When Hamilton of Holmhead was presented to her, she accused him of corrupting Lord Newton, who was a sober and a peaceable man till he fell in wi' him ; and she upbraided him for taking him to dine with Mr. Miller of Ballumbie when he was engaged to be at Pitlyal. He said he never prevented him dining at Pitlyal. She

---

[1] The lasses were the female servants, each of whom had a spinning-wheel, and when her share of the household work was done, she was bound to spin a *stent* or task for all the linens of the house ; from the finest damask to the coarsest sheeting was spun at home. There was great merriment in that room.

B

asked if he remembered meeting her at Ballumbie; to which he answered, No; yet he remembered not only the party, but he could tell every dish that was upon the table, and one of them was the best shoulder of mutton he ever saw, and turning to Lord Gillies, he whispered, " Surely the auld wife's telling a lee."

Miss Cathcart, Miss Kennedy, Mr. Rutherfurd—afterwards Lord Advocate and Lord Rutherfurd—and others, were all presented to her in due form. And when supper was announced, Lord Gillies gave her his arm down-stairs.

Mr. William Clerk offered his to Mrs. Gillies, that he might inquire the weight and qualifications of the heiress, and that they might get a seat near the old lady. He said he had fancied on his first entering the room that it was some one *dressed up*, but he now saw she was a very original person, and he wished to get acquainted with her. Mrs. Gillies told him the young lady had reddish hair, but he assured her that was no objection to him, for he had no dislike to red hair.

She alluded again to some stories of Lord Gillies's boyhood, and told him she had ploughed up the *Capernaum Park*, which he recollected to have been fine old grass.

Mr. Jeffrey now inquired what the people in her part of the country thought of the trial of the Queen. She could not tell him, but she would say what she herself had remarked on siclike proceedings : " Tak' a wreath of snaw, let it be never so white, and wash it through clean water, it will no' come out so pure as it gaed in, far less the dirty dubs the poor Queen has been drawn through."

Mr. Russell inquired if she possessed any relics of Prince Charles from the time he used to spin with the lasses.

" Yes," she said, " I have a *flech* that loupit aff him upon my aunty, the Lady Brax, when she was helping him on wi' his short gown ; my aunty rowed it up in a sheet of white paper, and she keepit it in the tea-canister, and she ca'd it aye the King's Flech ; and the Laird, honest man, when he wanted a cup of guid tea, sought aye a cup of the *Prince's mixture.*" This produced peals of laughter, and her Lady-ship laughed as heartily as any of them. When somewhat composed again, she looked across the table to Mr. Clerk, and offered to let him see it. "It is now set on the pivot of my watch, and a' the warks gae round the *flech* in place of turning on a diamond."

Lord Gillies thought this flight would certainly betray her, and remarked to Mr. Clerk that the flea must be painted on the watch, but Mr. Clerk said he had known of relics being kept of the Prince quite as extraordinary as a flae; that Mr. Murray of Simprim had a pocket handkerchief in which Prince Charles had blown his nose.

The Lady Pitlyal said her daughter did not value these things, and that she was resolved to leave it as a legacy to the Antiquarian Society.

Holmhead was rather amused with her originality, though he had not forgotten the attack. He said he would try if she was a real Jacobite, and he called out,

" Madam, I am going to propose a toast for ye !

" May the Scotch Thistle choke the Hanoverian Horse !"

" I wish I binna among the Whigs," she said.

" And whar wad ye be sae weel ? " retorted he.

" They murdered Dundee's son at Glasgow."

" There was nae great skaith," he replied ; " but ye maun drink my toast in a glass of this cauld punch, if ye be a true Jacobite."

"Aweel, aweel," said the Lady Pitlyal ; " as my auld friend Lady Christian Bruce was wont to say, ' The best way to get the better of temptation is just to yield to it ;'" and as she nodded to the toast and emptied the glass, Holmhead swore exultingly—" *Faith, she's true !* "

Supper passed over, and the carriages were announced.   The Lady Pitlyal took her leave with Mrs. Gillies.

Next day the town rang with the heiress of Pitlyal.   Mr. Clerk said he had never met with such an extraordinary old lady, "for not only is she amusing herself, but my brother John is like to expire when I relate her stories at second-hand."

He talked of nothing else for a week after, but the heiress, and the flea, and the rent-roll, and the old turreted house of Pitlyal, till at last his friends thought it would be right to undeceive him; but that was not so easily done, for when the Lord Chief Commissioner Adam hinted that it might be Miss Stirling, he said that was impossible, for Miss Stirling was sitting by the old lady the whole of the evening.

I WAS staying at Craigie with a very
pleasant party, and one day after dinner,
the Misses Guthrie proposed that I should
take in their father and mother.

Accordingly, a letter was written to the
Laird from his friend Mr. Dempster of
Dunnichen, to announce the visit of an
old acquaintance of his—a Mrs. Macallister
from Elgin, who was on her way to Edinburgh as a witness in Lord Fife's cause.
She had been staying some days at Dunnichen, and he was induced to give her
a billet on the well-known hospitality of
Craigie, because she was very amusing, a
great traveller, and was somewhat of an
oddity. He thought his friend would be
diverted with her, and hoped, for his sake,
he would pay her all the attention in his
power.

A horse was harnessed to an old caravan,

and it was driven up to the door with a great noise ; the door-bell rang, and the letter was sent in.

The Laird glanced it over.

" Where is the lady ?" he said, and the servant replied, " She was in her carriage at the door."

He started up in great haste, and went out to receive her.

" God bless me, Mrs. Macallister," he said, " are you standing in the hall ?" and he offered his arm to lead her into the drawing-room.

From the name and the object of the journey to Edinburgh, the representation was to have been that of a Highland lady, not of the very first grade of society ; but the unexpected appearance of Mr. Guthrie on the very threshold, the Laird, *par excellence,*—there were few like him then or now ; as a young man, he had made the tour of Europe when travelling was less common than in these days of railway speed,—the sight of the fine old man, his handsome countenance, his courtly bearing, and refined manners, and with all the formality and politeness of the old school, caused a total revolution in my personation. And Mrs. Macallister found herself all at once transposed into a very stiff old lady, *speaking English*, and her manner and deportment nearly on a level with that of the Laird himself.

Leaning on the arm of Mr. Guthrie, she was ushered into the drawing-room, and he presented her in due form to Mrs. Guthrie and every one of the assembled party.

A titter went round among those who were in the secret; and in order to regain the composure I had nearly lost, Mrs. Macallister was reduced to have recourse to a spasmodic pain in the side, in order to account for the shaking which the suppressed fit of laughter occasioned to her whole frame.

Mrs. Guthrie called for wine and other cordials, but Mrs. Macallister preferred the refreshment of a cup of coffee.

Still the laughing continued, and became the more irresistible to some of the party, by the very serious aspect of Sir

William Wiseman, who remonstrated on the impropriety of ridiculing an old person, even allowing her to be a little *outré* in her dress. And it was indeed sufficiently *outré*. A silk gown of flowered brocade, rich and stiff enough to have stood alone had there been nobody in it, and a most incongruous amalgamation of the ancient and the modern in the other articles of her apparel.

The Laird's equanimity was unshaken; he spoke of his friend Mr. Dempster and the probable issue of the Fife cause, and the unrelaxing politeness and gravity of his manner by degrees produced a state of calm.

He gave orders that Mrs. Macallister's horses should be well cared for, and remarked to Mrs. Guthrie that something must be wrong in his establishment, for when he went to the door to hand Mrs. Macallister out of her carriage he found her standing in the hall, and an old caravan with one horse at the door.

Mrs. Macallister explained that her carriage had broken down by the way from the state of the roads, and she was obliged to remain some hours at a place called Four-Mile House until even this conveyance could be procured; that she and her waiting-woman had been nearly knocked to pieces, and that this was the cause of the spasms and pain in her side.

Music and dancing were now proposed. The Laird and Mrs. Macallister went through a few steps of the *minuet de la cour;* Mrs. Warren and Sir William sat down to *écarté.* Some took up their work, and Lady Wiseman twisted a shawl round her head and performed some of the attitudes and songs of the Hindu singing-girls for the amusement of the party; while the Laird enjoyed a *tête-à-tête* at the fireside with his new friend.

She told him she had met a gentleman of his name in London, who was partner in a mercantile house with Mr. Chalmers of Auldbar.

"That is my son Charles," said the Laird.

"Another Mr. Guthrie I was introduced to at Gow's ball in Edinburgh,—a very facetious young gentleman. He paid me a great many compliments, and after leading me round the room and introducing me to some of his acquaintance, he called aloud to the music to play 'Such a pair was never seen.'"

Here the Laird laughed *con amore*, and cried out, "That is my son Sandy!"

Supper was now announced in the dining-room; the Laird offered his arm to Mrs. Macallister, and placed her beside himself at the table.

She now fell in fancy with his snuff-box, and offered to exchange with him, but he excused himself, saying, it was a keepsake from a deceased and valued friend, one whom Mrs. Macallister had perhaps heard of—the late Mr. Graham of Duntrune. She said she had known him, and esteemed him, and that very circumstance made her the more desirous to obtain it; it would be a memorandum of them both. The one she would give him was a very valuable one. It was the gift of an Indian chief to her late husband, Dr. Macallister, for an extraordinary cure he had performed on one of his children. Then, turning to Lady Wiseman, "You must have met with Dr. Macallister at Bombay. He was engaged in the compilation of a dictionary of the Gaelic language, which he did not live to finish." Lady Wiseman did not recollect.

She returned to the charge of the snuffbox, by placing her own very valuable gold one on the table, and putting the keepsake of the late Mr. Grahame of Duntrune in her pocket.

The Laird was annoyed beyond measure, but, too polite to express what he felt, he sat still in silent astonishment.

Mrs. Guthrie inquired if she had any family. "Four sons," was the answer. The eldest was high up in the India service. Sir William set about recollecting him, and inquired, "On what establishment?"

"Your second son?" said Mrs. Guthrie.

"Is a sailor, and very promising; and my third, a charming young man, is making a tour on the Continent."

Here Mrs. Macallister displayed a wish to change the subject; but the curiosity of Sir William was not satisfied until he said, "And where is your youngest son, Mrs. Macallister?"

It was no easy matter to account for so many "grown gentlemen."

"My youngest son is——God knows where," and here she was seized with an involuntary laugh, and again had recourse to the spasmodic pain, while the simple and kind-hearted Sir William, upbraiding himself for so heedlessly touching such a tender chord, covered his face with his handkerchief and wept.

At eleven o'clock Miss Guthrie offered to light Mrs. Macallister to her room, but she waved aside the proffered arm, and told the Laird that Mr. Dempster had always conducted her to the door of her apartment himself, kissed her when he bade good-night, and assured her that his good friend Craigie would not be behind him in point of gallantry.

The Laird accordingly held out his arm, led her up-stairs, and at the door of her chamber, when she took off her bonnet to conclude the scene, as the well-known features met his eyes, he stood for some seconds transfixed to the spot. Then suddenly relaxing from his formality, he laughed till the tears came into his eyes, and the first words he spoke were, "Now, Clemy, give me back my snuff-box."

Another evening, when Lady Hunter and her daughter (now Mrs. Basil Hall) were there, the Laird expressed a fancy to give them a benefit of the same kind that had been productive of so much pleasure to himself. A letter was therefore composed and delivered to him, just as the table-cloth was removed after dinner.

He looked at the direction, and examined the seal in a manner that proved him to be a most excellent actor. "An earl's coronet," he said in an audible whisper, and then looking over its contents, read aloud a letter from Lord North-esk, purporting that the Lady Catherine Howard had come down to Scotland for the express purpose of visiting the scenes and illustrating some of Sir Walter Scott's novels; that she had been paying a visit at Ethie, whence he had carried her to the Red Head, and shown her the Auchmithie fishers. He now begged leave to introduce her at Craigie, and requested his friend Mr. Guthrie would give her all the information in his power respecting "the Antiquary," who, she had been told by Sir Walter himself, was a Mr. George Constable, of a place called the Wallace, somewhere near Dundee.

The letter was handed round and severally commented on, and Lady Catherine Howard was expected to follow her *avant-coureur* in the course of an hour.

Soon after the ladies returned to the drawing-room, the noise of carriage-wheels and a loud knock at the door announced the arrival of the distinguished stranger.

Mr. Guthrie, delighted with the part he had to play, hastened to hand her Ladyship from the carriage. He joined me in the next room, but I was waiting for an apron to complete the costume of Lady

Catherine Howard. No apron was to be found, nor anything in the shape of one, and here was a dilemma which could not easily be got over, as the dress was altogether incomplete without one.

A net frock, however, lay on the table, round the skirt of which Miss Hunter had been working a lace pattern for her friend Miss Rose Guthrie. Lady Catherine fearlessly tied it round her waist, and, leaning on the arm of Mr. Guthrie, walked into the drawing-room.

There she was presented to the circle, but most particularly to Lady Hunter, with whom she fell into a very interesting conversation about Spain, which they had both visited; indeed Lady Hunter had lived there for years.

Many names were mentioned well known to each other, both abroad and at home; they became friends as if they had been linked together for years, while the Laird now and then chimed in the name of his friend Lord Lansdowne, his son the late Lord, and asked some information concerning the lineage of Norfolk and Suffolk, and the blood of the Howards. They played a rubber, and there was music, but Lady Catherine reserved her praise till Miss Hunter sat down to the instrument.

The young ladies' work was commented on, and after various observations she held up the corner of her apron, saying it was the work of Lady Elizabeth Carnegie, which had been finished and presented to her during her visit to Ethie.

Miss Hunter looked at it, and remarked that it was the same pattern of the one she was working for Miss Rose Guthrie, and "See, Rose," she added, "there is a joining across that leaf exactly like the one I am doing for you; is not that very curious?"

Lady Catherine spoke of the object which had induced her to come to Scotland, and Lady Hunter said she would give her an introduction to Sir James Hall of Dunglass, on whose property lies the scene of Wolf's Crag in the *Bride of Lammermoor*. And she added, "There are many very interesting scenes in and about Edinburgh which are well worth visiting. I will give your Ladyship a letter to my brother, Sir William Arbuthnot, present Lord Provost of Edinburgh, who will be happy to show you everything that is to be seen."

The supper tray was brought in with some warm dishes; and laying aside her bonnet to eat the wing of a roast chicken, the vision of Lady Catherine Howard vanished as if by magic.

Lady Hunter gazed for a moment as if a spirit had passed before her, started from her chair, then rushed forward with open arms, kissed and embraced the humble individual who filled her chair.

———

ANOTHER evening Miss Guthrie requested me to introduce my old lady to Captain Alexander Lindsay, a son of the late Laird of Kinblethmont, and brother to the present Mr. Lindsay Carnegie, and Mr. Sandford, the late Sir Daniel Sandford.

She came as a Mrs. Ramsay Speldin, an old sweetheart of the Laird's, and was welcomed by Mrs. Guthrie as a friend of the family. The young people hailed her as a perfectly delightful old lady, and an original of the pure Scottish character, and to the Laird she was endeared by a thousand pleasing recollections.

He placed her beside himself on the sofa, and they talked of the days gone by —before the green parks of Craigie were redeemed from the muir of Gotterston, and ere there was a tree planted between the auld house of Craigie and the castle of Claypotts.

She spoke of the "gude auld times, when the laird of Fintry widna gi'e his youngest dochter to Abercairney, but tell'd him to tak' them as God had gi'en them to him, or want."

"And do you mind," she continued, "the grand ploys we had at the Middleton; and hoo Mrs. Scott of Gilhorn used to grind lilts out o' an auld kist to wauken her visitors i' the mornin'?

"And some o' them didna like it sair,

though nane o' them had courage to tell her sae, but Anny Graham o' Duntrune.

" ' Lord forgie ye,' said Mrs. Scott, ' ye'll no gae to Heaven, if ye dinna like music;' but Anny was never at a loss for an answer, and she said, ' Mrs. Scott, Heaven's no' the place I take it to be, if there be auld wives in it playing on hand-organs.' "

Many a story did Mrs. Ramsay tell. The party drew their chairs close to the sofa, and many a joke she related, till the room rung again with the merriment, and the Laird in ecstasy caught her round the waist, exclaiming, " Oh ! ye are a canty wifie."

The strangers seemed to think so too ; they absolutely hung upon her, and she danced reels, first with the one, and then with the other, till the entrance of a servant with the newspapers produced a seasonable calm.

They lay, however, untouched upon the table till Mrs. Ramsay requested some one to read over the claims that were

putting in for the King's Coronation, and
see if there was any mention of hers.

"What is your claim?" said Mr. Sandford.

"To pyke the King's teeth," was the
reply.

"You will think it very singular," said
Mr. Guthrie, "that I never heard of it
before; will you tell us how it originated?"

"It was in the time of James the
First," she said. "That monarch cam'
to pay a visit to the monks of Arbroath,
and they brought him to Ferryden to eat
a fish dinner at the house of ane o' my
forefathers. The family name, ye ken,
was Speldin, and the dried fish was ca'd
after them.

"The king was well satisfied wi' a'
thing that was done to honour him. He
was a very polished prince, and when he
had eaten his dinner he turned round to
the lady and sought a preen to pyke his
teeth.

"And the lady took a fish-bane, wiped
it clean, and ga'e it to the king; and

after he had cleaned his teeth wi' it, he said, ' 𝔗𝔥𝔢𝔶'𝔯𝔢 𝔴𝔢𝔢𝔩 𝔭𝔶𝔨𝔦𝔱.'

" ' And henceforth,' continued he, ' the Speldins of Ferryden shall pyke the king's teeth at the Coronation. And it shall be done wi' a fish-bone, and a pearl out o' the Southesk on the end of it. And their crest shall be a lion's head wi' the teeth displayed, and the motto shall be *weel pykit.'* "

Mr. Sandford read over the claims, but there was no notice given of the Speldins.

" We maun just ha'e patience," said Mrs. Speldin, " and nae doubt it will appear in the next newspaper."

Some one inquired who was the present representative.

" It's me," replied Mrs. Speldin ; " and I mean to perform the office mysel'. The estate wad ha'e been mine too, had it existed ; but Neptune, ye ken, is an ill neighbour, and the sea has washed it a' awa but a sand bunker or twa, and the house I bide in at Ferryden."

At supper every one was eager to have a seat near Mrs. Speldin. She had a universal acquaintance, and she even knew Mr. Sandford's mother, when he told her that her name was Catherine Douglas. Mr. Sandford had in his own mind composed a letter to Sir Walter Scott, which was to have been written and despatched on the morrow, giving an account of this fine specimen of the true Scottish character whom he had met in the county of Angus.

We meant to carry on the deception next morning, but the Laird was too happy for concealment. Before the door closed on the good-night of the ladies, he had disclosed the secret, and before we reached the top of the stairs, the gentlemen were scampering at our heels like a pack of hounds in full cry.

I WENT with Lord Gillies and Mrs. Gillies to spend the Christmas holidays at Tulliallan. We met Admiral and Mrs. Fleming, Mr. and Mrs. Keay of Snaigow, Mr. John Murray (afterwards Lord Murray), Mr. and Mrs. Russell, Mr. Thomas Thomson, etc.—a very pleasant party.

Lady Keith wished me to *take in* Count Flahault, but no feasible means could be devised, till one day that a robbery had been committed in the neighbourhood. Two boys were accused, named John Murray and Alexander Jamieson ; the former had escaped, but the other was taken up, and brought to be examined before the Justices of the Peace assembled at the Castle.

It was suggested that I should come in form of the mother of one of these lads. Accordingly, a costume was borrowed from the dairymaid, and I was speedily transformed into the character of Mrs. Jamieson, who desired to speak with some of the gentlemen that were taking the precognition.

I cannot say that I felt altogether comfortable when I was ushered into an apartment among a motley group of witnesses, and was desired to wait until I was called up-stairs; but Lady Keith arranged that I should not have long to wait, and desired the servant to bring Mrs. Jamieson into the corridor. The drawing-rooms opened to it, and the doors being left open, the party within could hear all that passed.

Count Flahault and Admiral Fleming came from the justice-room, and the latter demanded in an angry tone, " What is your business ?"

" I am the mither of Alexander Jamieson, and am come to see if you will let off my son."

" The devil you are," said the Admiral; " your son is a young thief, and deserves to be hanged."

" I winna say."

" Because you know very well that you have brought him very ill up, and I suppose you encourage him to steal for you."

"God forgi'e ye," said Mrs. Jamieson ; "it's the like o' you that ha'e ruined him. He was a gude weel-living lad afore ye sent him to Bridewell."

"What !" said Count Flahault, " has your son been in Bridewell ? "

No answer.

" I say," said the Count, " has your son been in Bridewell ? "

Still no answer.

The Count then repeated slowly and distinctly—

" Has your son ever been in Bridewell ? "

" Yes."

" For what was he sent to Bridewell ? '

" For nae great affair."

" Tell instantly," said the Admiral, " for what he was sent to Bridewell ? "

" For nae ither thing, but just because he whuppit a shawl off a stand, and gied it till 's sweetheart."

"Ay," said the Admiral; "and pray how long has your son been in Bridewell? —speak out."

"Sax weeks, and he cam' out a great deal waur than he gaed in."

"I have not the smallest doubt of that," said the Admiral; "I believe you speak the truth now;" and returning to the justice-room, he taxed the boy with having been in Bridewell, and received an answer in the affirmative.

The Count then asked what brought her. "I am come to mak' ye an offer," replied the persevering Mrs. Jamieson.

"What kind of an offer?" said the Count, with a smile between compassion and contempt.

"I ken," said Mrs. Jamieson, "you would like very weel to get a haud o' John Murray, and if ye'll let off my son, I'se engage to get John Murray to you this very night."

"So you know where John Murray is, do you?" and he went back to the justice-room to relate the further particulars.

Lady Keith by this time became fearful

of mixing up the false witness with the true, and calling to the Count, she said, " For God's sake, Charles, give that poor woman half-a-crown, and send her away. I cannot bear to see her standing there."

The Count desired the weeping Mrs. Jamieson to go home—an order which she very slowly set about obeying—hesitating and turning round to plead her cause every now and then.

The Count, however, was resolute, and gently laying a hand on each shoulder, he marched her before him, and opening the outer door, he put half-a-crown into her hand, and pushed her out, she in the meantime upbraiding him with having the heart of Pharaoh, that could turn a poor woman to the door in sic a night.

The Count was delighted with the *dénouement;* but upbraided Lady Keith with hurrying on the conclusion.

" Why did you not let me be more taken in ?" he said ; " and why did Mrs. Jamieson conclude the scene so soon ? She shall be brought back again, and we shall have a little fun with Keay."

After dinner, therefore, Mrs. Jamieson's return was announced. She was ordered to the dining-room door, and Mr. Keay was appointed to hear her statement.

She detailed, in the most pathetic terms, how Sandy Jamieson was the support of her old age, and that she came to petition for his being released.

Mr. Keay endeavoured to soothe her, spoke kindly, bade her be comforted, assured her that her son would be taken care of as far as he was concerned, but that he could not release him.

"I ken weel what kind o' care ye will tak' o' him," she said.

"What do you mean, my good woman?" returned Mr. Keay.

"I ken," said Mrs. Jamieson, "you're gaen to mak' a ploy o' hangin' him the nicht, and ye've got Edinburgh judges in the house, and I saw them scrapin' a tree as I cam' up the gait;" and she wept bitterly, and her grief became clamorous, and she would not move until she should see her son.

Mr. Keay recollected having seen two

of the foresters in the morning rubbing the lichens off some old oaks on the lawn ; but it was impossible to convince Mrs. Jamieson that it could be for any other purpose but that of preparing a gallows for her son. He returned to the dining-room to communicate to the party the state she was in, and the delusion under which she laboured.

" Give her half-a-crown, Keay," said the Count; "and do you, Admiral, give her as much, and she'll go home."

" I would see her hanged first," replied the Admiral ; but Mr. Keay returned to the comfort of the distressed, and taking her kindly by the hand, slipped half-a-crown into it.

" What is that?" said she, throwing down the money; "it is the price of blood, and it shall never be said that Janet Jamieson sell'd her bairn's blood for half-a-crown."

" You mistake, my good woman," said Mr. Keay, " it is not the price of blood. I assure you your son is quite safe ; he is gone to Culross in a cart."

"To Culross in a cart!" shrieked Mrs. Jamieson. "I winna stir from this house till ye bring him back again."

Mr. Keay's patience was now exhausted, and the more especially when he heard shouts of merriment from the dining-room. "If you don't speedily take yourself off, you will be turned out. Better, therefore, take the half-crown, and trust me there will no harm happen to your son to-night;" saying which, he returned into the dining-room, and shut the door upon the distressed mother.

By the time the gentlemen joined the ladies in the drawing-room, a hole had been drilled through each of the half-crowns, and they were suspended round the neck of their new proprietor.

Some months afterwards I happened to go with some strangers to see the new jail in Edinburgh. The prisoners were amusing themselves in their airing-ground.

"That," said the jailer, pointing to a young man, "is the most hardened and incorrigible offender we have." I inquired his name, and he said it was John Murray.

FROM Tulliallan we removed to Raith, to bring in the New Year. A very brilliant party was assembled. The gentlemen enjoyed the pleasures of the *battue* in the mornings, and we sat down to dinner upwards of twenty every day.

The party consisted of Mr. and Mrs. Ferguson, Sir Ronald and Miss Ferguson, Mr. and Mrs. Henry Ferguson (now Sir Henry and Lady Davie), Mr. and Mrs. Michael Angelo Taylor, Lord Gillies and Mrs. Gillies, Mr. and Mrs. Russell, the Marquis of Tweeddale and his brothers Lords John and Thomas Hay, Lord Maitland, the present Lord Lauderdale, and the Honourable Captain Maitland, Count Flahault, Lord Duncan (the present Lord Camperdown), Mr. John Murray, and though last, not least, the Honourable John Elliot, the very life and soul of the

Raith.

party. He was the universal favourite, and was altogether a delightful person, full of anecdote, and a mimic of the first water.

Sir Ronald gave us personations of a certain Provost, and Mr. Murray gave specimens of all the Judges on the bench; and after we had been some days together, Mr. Ferguson announced the expectation of a visit of the Lady Pitlyal, and expressed his regret that I was engaged to a ball at Lord Rosslyn's.

Her Ladyship arrived just as dinner was announced, having remained in Kirkcaldy by the advice of her coachman till after dark, " as he said there was a great gathering of thoughtless young men at Raith, and there was to be a battle wi' the Ephesians, and he thought we had better keep out o' harm's way."

Lord Gillies offered his arm to the dining-room, and placed her at table between himself and Mr. Elliot.

She expressed great disappointment in not finding Lord Lauderdale of the party. " I understood he was to be at Raith," she

said, "and I wanted to consult him on a
piece of business of great importance both
to myself and the nation."

Mr. Elliot pressed her to take Maras-
chino, till Lord Gillies was obliged to tell
him he knew the Lady Pitlyal was a very
abstemious person, and that she never
took anything but a glass of wine at
dinner. She spoke to him of the estate of
Melgund, and of its having been the residence of Cardinal Bethune.

He believed it was rather a good place,
and inquired if she knew it well.

She said she kenned a' the land there-
about, frae the south side of Seidlaw to
the north o' the Grampians; and she told
him how a living lobster had fallen out of
a cadger's creel up about the parish of
Lintrathen, and how a Highlandman had
picked it up and carried it to the minister,
and how the minister put on his spectacles
to see what kind of a beast it was, and
after lang examination, and mony a refer-
ence to the Bible, he pronounced it to be
either an *elephant* or a *turtle-dove*.

Mr. Elliot in his turn related how a seafaring friend of his, in giving an order for provisioning the ship, said, " I am resolved to have a *cow, for I am very fond of new-laid eggs.*"

He then told her that a young lady had taken his purse the night before, and he would refer to the Lady Pitlyal what punishment should be awarded.

She said she would give the same judgment that the Bellman of Arbroath did on a like occasion, when he happened to be the finder of it himsel':—

" John Elliot's lost his purse,
And his money, which is worse ;
Them that's found it let them keep it,
Them that's tint it, let them seek it."

When dinner was removed, and the domestics were withdrawn, she recurred again to her regret at missing Lord Lauderdale, as it was of great consequence to her to have her bill brought in this session.

Mr. Ferguson begged to know the nature of the bill, as some of the party present might perhaps be of use to her.

She said it concerned a charter which

had lately been discovered in the garret of Pitlyal; it was a grant from James the Fifth, that the leeches of the loch of Pitlyal should become a monopoly; and she wished Lord Lauderdale to bring in a bill obliging the king and all the heads of the nation to use the Pitlyal leeches.

Lord Tweeddale said he would be happy to lay it before the peers, and Sir Ronald was sure his friend Mr. Taylor would bring it into the House of Commons.

Lord Gillies begged she would explain the origin of the charter.

She said "the king was on a hunting party in Strathmore, and he was thrown from his horse and ta'en up for dead; that leeches were got from the loch of Pitlyal and applied to his head, and he recovered; and when he cam' till himsel' he speered at some o' the bystanders what like his head was, and the gudeman of that place said there was a muckle clour upon 't. '*Muckle clour*,' says the king; 'henceforth this place shall be called Muckle Clour, and the land, gudeman, shall be your ain.'"

Baith.

"The place was since sell'd to an ancestor of Lady Keith's; it is now ca'd Meikleour, ye ken, Count; and the king said, 'Ye shall bear the leeches on your shield, and I bind myself and my subjects to make use of them in need.'

"The richt o' the leeches wasna disposed o' when Mickleclour was sell'd; but for mair than a century the charter has been amissing, and leeches have been ta'en out o' ither lochs, and great quantities have been brought over from Holland; and now it will na be an easy thing to bring back the monopoly."

Mr. Taylor was doubtful how such a thing could be done; nor could he distinctly see by what right she could expect it.

Mr. Russell thought it might be a right of the same kind that secures thirlage to a mill.

Lord Duncan interrupted the subject of right by stating that he had many times been at Pitlyal, and had heard her Ladyship speak a great deal about the loch leeches, but he would like just to be informed how she had been in the practice of catching them.

"Oh Robert, Robert!" replied her Lady-ship reproachfully, " mony ane speers the road they ken. I've seen you aft'ner than ance wade into the water and come out wi' them sticking on your legs."

The cause was triumphant; his Lord-ship was fairly cheered into his recollec-tion, but Mr. Taylor could not be made to understand it, and no one could assume sufficient gravity to explain.

As soon as a hearing could be obtained, Count Flahault inquired after the health of the Rosebud.

" She's very weel, and shortly to be married," replied her Ladyship.

" To whom, may I beg leave to ask ?"

" To the Prince of Monaco."

" A friend of mine," said the Count; but the name was not familiar to any of the rest of the party.

" I'll gi'e ye a Scotch mark," she said to Mr. Ferguson; " it was his father that thought a' the lamps in London had been lighted up in honour of his arrival, and as he drove through the city he exclaimed with delight, ' I 've often heard the English was a polite nation, but this is too much.' I believe," she added, " my Jean will be a great match for him, for his principality is the very smallest in Italy; it lies, I believe, on the shore of the Mediterranean."

The Count bit his lip. " It does," said he, " and the gentleman is my particular friend; he is now the "— I forget the name.

In the drawing-room Mr. Elliot hastened to the side of his new friend, and many was the story they successively told.

" You carry the leeches on your shield?" said Mr. Elliot.

" And the lion for the crest. I am the lion," she replied.

" I was once a hare myself," returned he; and he began a story he had told the night before—how he had acted the part of a hare, to the astonishment of an old gentleman in the neighbourhood of Minto. Before the end of it, however, he caught the expression of the lady's eye, and lifting up the veil which shaded her features, exclaimed—" Now I have found the Lion of Pitlyal."

Dinner Party
at Lord
Gillies's.

Sir Walter Scott expressed a wish to see a personation, and Lord Gillies made a party for the purpose, among whom were Sir Walter and Miss Scott, Sir Henry and Lady Jardine, the Lord Chief Commissioner and Miss Adam, Doctor Coventry, the Chief Baron Sir Samuel Shepherd, and others.

Among other things that afforded subject of conversation was the fancy ball of the night before; the various dresses and characters were commented on, and among them the inconsistent conduct of a black knight, who had thrown down the gauntlet without waiting to see who would pick it up. The knight was said to be young Mr. T——.

The dinner passed very pleasantly, as

all Lord Gillies's dinners do; and when we returned to the drawing-room I bade good-night to the ladies.

The Misses Carnegy and their old friend Mrs. Arbuthnott of Balwylie came to tea.

With all the ladies, except Lady Jardine and Miss Scott, Mrs. Arbuthnott was intimately acquainted. To them, therefore, she was now by Mrs. Gillies particularly introduced.

Lady Jardine whispered to Mrs. Gillies, " What a beautifully dressed old lady; her clothes are so handsome, and so suitable to her time of life, and at the same time fashionable and ladylike. I wish some old ladies in this town would only take example by it."

The gown was a dark silk, made up to the throat, and with sleeves to the wrist. A pure white gauze handkerchief pinned tight over it, an apron of clear white muslin trimmed with point lace, and a cap of point with bows of white satin ribbon; a green shade and French grey kid gloves seamed with black silk.

Mrs. Gillies hoped she was to have the pleasure of seeing the rest of Mrs. Arbuthnott's family. To which she replied that they would all be here, but that they were dining out.

Miss Adam inquired how many of her family had come up with her.

" There is the Laird," she said, " my eldest son, and the three orphans left to my care by my second son, and there's our right-hand man and governor, James Dalgetty."

" The young men," she continued, " wanted a little amusement, and they cam' up to the Fancy Ball. The Laird had to attend a meeting of the Antiquarian Society, and I thought I might as weel tak' the opportunity to come and see my friends."

" Your grandsons will be grown out of my acquaintance," said Miss Adam.

" They're fine handsome young men," was the reply ; " and Charles, the youngest of them, is the life and spirit of the whole house. He's a jewel of a creature, and the very image of his father."

"How did they like the ball?" inquired Miss Scott.

"Extraordinary weel; and Charles went in the dress of a black knight."

"Was it your grandson then, Mrs. Arbuthnott," continued Miss Scott, "that was the black knight? I am delighted to hear you say so. It destroyed the romance of the thing altogether when we were told it was the son of Mr. T——."

The gentlemen now entered the drawing-room. All who were previously acquainted with Mrs. Arbuthnott expressed their delight at meeting her, and she became in a high degree animated by the sight of so many old friends.

The Lord Chief Commissioner, claiming the privilege of an old sweetheart, sat down beside her on the sofa, and Sir Walter Scott, though a new acquaintance, placed himself by her on the other side.

"Do you know, papa," said Miss Scott, "that Mrs. Arbuthnott's grandson was the black knight?"

"And poor Charles got a sad fright,"

continued Mrs. Arbuthnott; "he did very weel till he threw down the glove, but syne he lost his presence o' mind a'thegither."

"I am afraid," said Sir Walter, "it is no uncommon thing for knights in his situation to lose their presence of mind."

"Where are the rest of your party, Mrs. Arbuthnott?" now inquired Lord Gillies.

"They'll be here presently, my Lord; but the Laird is gone to a meeting of the Antiquarians, and the young men will come as soon as their dinner party breaks up." Then turning to Sir Walter, "I am sure you had our Laird in your e'e when you drew the character of Monkbarns."

"No," replied Sir Walter; "but I had in my eye a very old and respected friend of my own, and one with whom I daresay you, Mrs. Arbuthnott, were acquainted,— the late Mr. George Constable of Wallace, near Dundee."

"I kenned him weel," said Mrs. Arbuthnott, "and his twa sisters that lived wi' him, Jean and Christian, and I've been in the blue-chamber of his *Hospitium;* but I think," she continued, "our Laird is the likest to Monkbarns o' the twa. He's at the Antiquarian Society the night, presenting a great curiosity that was found in a quarry of mica-slate in the hill at the back of Balwylic. He's sair ta'en up about it, and puzzled to think what substance it may be; but James Dalgetty, wha's never at a loss either for the name or the nature of onything under the sun, says it's just Noah's auld wig that blew aff yon time he put his head out of the window of the ark to look after his corbie messenger."

James Dalgetty and his opinion gave subject of much merriment to the company; but Doctor Coventry thought there was nothing so very ludicrous in the remark, for in that kind of slate there are frequently found substances resembling hairs.

Lord Gillies presented Doctor Coventry to Mrs. Arbuthnott as the well-known Professor of Agriculture, and they entered on a conversation respecting soils. She

Mystifications.

described those of Balwylie, and the particular properties of the *Surroch Park*, which James Dalgetty curses every time it's spoken about, and says, " It greets a' winter, and girns a' simmer."

The Doctor rubbed his hands with delight, and said that was the most perfect description of cold wet land he had ever heard of; and Sir Walter expressed a wish to cultivate the acquaintance of James Dalgetty, and extorted a promise from Mrs. Arbuthnott that she would visit Abbotsford, and bring James with her. "I have a James Dalgetty of my own," continued Sir Walter, " that governs me just as yours does you."

Lady Ann and Mr. Wharton Duff and their daughter were announced, and introduced to Mrs. Arbuthnott.

Lady Ann was remarkably *spirituelle*, possessed a great talent for fun and humour, spoke the Scotch fluently, and entered the lists at once with Mrs. Arbuthnott. Many a good story she told; not only witty herself, but, as Falstaff says, she was also the cause of wit in others

—and was altogether a very delightful person.

Mrs. Arbuthnott inquired if she had heard what had happened to a laird on Deeside, when he was salmon-fishing short syne.

"What laird?" said Lady Ann.

"One that shall be nameless for the present," continued Mrs. Arbuthnott; "but the first bite nearly whummeled him into the water. 'Gi'e him line,' cried Willy Bruce the fisher; 'that chield maun ha'e play.'

"And sure enough the laird ga'e him line; three days and twa nights he warstled wi' the beast, and there wasna a bush, nor the stump o' an auld tree, a' the way between the Falls of the Feuch and the Linn o' Dee, that he didna mak' steppin'-stanes o'. At length the line broke, and down cam' the laird. 'The devil's got the hook,' he cried, and up again he couldna rise.

"A' body wonders if he saw onything, and some say it was the auld Abbot of Arbroath, that used to dress himsel' iu a

white coat and a curled wig, to gar folk
believe he was the Laird o' Seton, when
there was ony ploy gaen on that wasna
just suitable for a monk's cowl to be seen
in.

"He was doomed to haunt the rivers for
a thousand years afore he should get into
purgatory.

"But Willy Bruce swears it was naething but a muckle salmon that he's
kenned in the water these twenty years,
and the fishers ca'd him William the Con-
queror, because he managed aye to brak
their lines; but be that as it may, the
laird got sic a fleg that he was carried
hame in a raging fever, and he's keepit
his bed aye sin syne."

"I know where you are now," exclaimed
Lady Ann Duff, and she began to relate a
pendant to this history about the Laird of
Abergeldie. But the laughter caused by
the downfal of the salmon-fishing laird,
only received a fresh impulse from this
interruption.

Mr. Henry Jardine and his sister were
announced; the former recognised a friend

beneath the green shade, and his smile was returned by Mrs. Arbuthnott.

Dinner Party at Lord Gillies's.

He was a friend of Charles's, and had been at Balwylie.

At ten, Sir Walter and Miss Scott took leave, with a promise that they should visit each other; and bending down to the ear of Mrs. Arbuthnott, Sir Walter addressed her in these words: "Awa! awa! the deil's ower grit wi' you."

I once got half-a-crown from Sir William Fettes when he was dining with a few friends at his sister, Mrs. Bruce's.

Evening at Mrs. Bruce's.

She and Lady Fettes put it into my head to ask charity from him, in the character of the daughter of an old companion of his, whose name was Sandy Reid. And whether Sandy Reid ever had a daughter was nothing to the purpose. Sir William had lost sight of the man, and I had no previous knowledge that ever such a person was in existence.

Dressed in a smart bonnet and shawl

belonging to Lord Gillies's housekeeper, I boldly rung the door-bell, and demanded of the servant if I could get a word of Sir William.

On the message being carried up-stairs, the ladies desired that the person who wished to speak with Sir William might be shown into Mrs. Bruce's dressing-room, where behind the window-curtains were stationed a merry party of some half-a-dozen listeners.

Enter Sir William.

" Well, my good woman, what is your business with me ? "

" To ask your help, sir, in behalf of the widow and the fatherless."

" And pray who are you ? "

" I am the daughter of ane Sandy Reid, who was weel kenned to your honour ; his father lived next door to your father in the Canongate."

" Ay, are you the daughter of Sandy Reid ? "

" I am proud to say sae."

" And what has reduced you to this plight, my good woman ? "

"Just an ill marriage, Sir William.'

"I am sorry for that; but you say you are a widow."

"I am no' just a widow; but my husband has run aff wi' anither woman."

"That is very unfortunate; but what is your husband?"

"A soldier, sir."

"An officer of the soldiers you mean, I suppose?"

"Na, na, Sir William; he is but a single soldier."

"And did Sandy Reid's daughter marry a single soldier?"

Weeping—"It is o'er true, Sir William; but he was a bonny man, and I ne'er thought he would forsake me."

"And did your father consent to your marrying a single soldier?"

"Oh, no, Sir William; but it was ordained."

"Have you any family, or any means of living?"

"I have five boys; and I wash and iron, and do all I can to get bread to them."

"Where do you live?"

"In Elder Street."

"In Elder Street! that seems to me rather an expensive part of the town for a person in your circumstances."

"It is but a garret, sir, up four pair of stairs."

"Are any of your children at school?"

"No, sir; but the eldest is in Provost Manderson's shop, who has been very kind to him, and ta'en him aff my hand. And the second is a prentice to a tobacconist; and (here weeping bitterly) the rest are in the house, for I have neither decent claes to put upon them, nor siller to send them to the schule; and this is Saturday night, and no sae muckle meat within the door as put by the Sabbath-day."

"I am sorry for you, and grieved to see Sandy Reid's daughter come to this; but you must be sensible, that for a person in your situation, your present dress is rather too showy and extravagant."

"That's true, Sir William; but gentle servants are no' civil to poor folk when they come ill-dressed."

" I believe, indeed, that is too true, but your dress is quite unsuitable."

" Indeed, Sir William, I borrowed this bonnet and shawl from a gentleman's housekeeper, just for the purpose of waiting upon you, for I am in great want."

" Well, there is half-a-crown to help you in the meantime; and I will inquire at Provost Manderson about you on Monday, and if you be speaking the truth, I will see and get your children into some of the Hospitals."

Here the party broke out from behind the curtains.

ANTERIOR to any of the forementioned scenes, we had many similar ones at Kelly and Duntrune, where a friendly intercourse subsisted between the families.

Kelly, near Arbroath, was the delightful residence of the Honourable Colonel and Mrs. Ramsay, with its fine old castle, its gardens and romantic Den, where were reared a family of thirteen promising children, and where good taste and genuine hospitality prevailed. The actress of these *Mystifications* was sometimes induced to play a merry scene, to amuse the children as well as their parents. Once she personated the character of a French governess, whose family had suffered in the Revolution, and the young people were cautioned to be on their good behaviour; the lady could not speak English, and she made them understand that they were to begin the lessons by pronouncing every word as she did. Five or six of the elder children stood up before this awful lady ; they were very timid, very respectful, and repeated with great gravity, and much distortion of their little mouths, every word as she spoke it. Then followed a dancing lesson; then a drill, at the end of which they were commanded to kneel on the left knee, when Madame de Brujack gave the nearest one a push that laid them all flat on the floor. . It was a joyous scene; such peals of laughter from old and young when they discovered the formidable French lady was only their own familiar friend. Colonel and Mrs. Ramsay, with the brother of the Colonel, General James Ramsay, spent some Christmas holidays at Duntrune, where they were joined by the Miss Grahams of Balmure. One evening we all drove to the theatre in Dundee, and on our return, just before supper, Lady Wilson was announced,— the mother of Sir Robert Wilson, who helped the French Emperor's escape from the Prison of Vincennes. She came to

The French Governess.

solicit from the brothers a special introduction to Lord Panmure, stating that her son-in-law would have given her a letter, but he had gone abroad—here some of the party heard the Colonel whisper to his brother, "*That's Perceval; he married her daughter.*" Her Ladyship wished for some particular piece of information which Lord Panmure could give, and for which she had travelled all the way from Charleton at this inclement season. The deception lasted till supper was announced, when Lady Wilson retired to rest.

[FEW are now alive who shared or assisted in these joyous scenes, and the Mystifier, at an advanced age, waits in humble reliance the certainty of her summons.

C. S. G.

DUNTRUNE, *December* 1868.]

THE FUTURE.

BLESSED shades of the past,
In the future I see ye, so fair!
   Ties that were nearest,
   Forms that were dearest,
The truest and fondest are there.

   They were flowerets of earth,
That are blooming in heaven, so fair!
   And the stately tree,
   Spreading wide and free,
The sheaves that were ripened are there.

   The tear-drop that trembled
In pity's meek eye; and the prayer,
   Faith of the purest,
   Hope that was surest,
The love all-enduring, are there.

   And the loved, the beloved
Whose life made existence so fair!
   The soft seraph voice
   Bade the lowly rejoice,
Is heard in sweet harmony there.

TO THE HEIRESS OF PITLYAL.

DEAR ROSEBUD,

       I 'm tired of a bachelor life,
And have taken the field in pursuit of a wife;
Of all the young ladies I 've viewed in succes-
    sion,
You 've made on my soul the most lasting im-
    pression;
And it is not that form, nor those features I
    prize,
But the light of good-humour that beams in
    those eyes,
And the sweet smile of kindness that meets
    my attentions,
Spur me on at this moment to state my pre-
    tensions.

My family, you know, is both ancient and
    good,
We can trace our descent in a line from the
    Flood,

And the flock of grey geese on the pond in
    my park,
Genealogists prove have been hatched in the
    ark.
Indeed, among other rare things I can show a
Bobwig that belonged to old commodore
    Noah !

    My fortune is ample,—a rent-roll quite
        clear,
Of arable acres ten thousand a year ;
What with peats, and hill pasture, and kelp
    on the shore,
I may state it with safety at three hundred
    more.

    I have ten serving damsels, and as many
        men,
Who have lived in the castle threescore years
    and ten ;
My hounds and my hawks are in numbers
    past counting,
Old racers past running, old hunters past
    mounting ;
But still I have twenty good steeds in my
    stable,
Nine bays and four chestnuts, six greys and
    one sable ;

I 've two coaches, three chariots, and one
     sedan chair,
With some trifling exceptions no worse for the
     wear ;
A few hundreds of spiders their threads have
     been twining,
And the moths and the mice have their nests
     in the lining.

     Now to turn out these settlers so late in
         the season,
Seems to me against nature, if not against
     reason ;
So to obviate this, the best thing I can do
Is to make Whippy[1] send down a pillion for
     you.

     There 's a gay riding dress which my aunt
         Lady Marles
Had sent her from London to wait on Prince
     Charles ;
'Tis of blue *peau de soie*, lined with *couleur
     de rose*,
With a helmet and feathers, and tassels, and
     bows ;

        [1] A celebrated London saddler.

If to my proposal you start no objection,
The habit may suit both your taste and com-
plexion.

    Then, my bride, I will mount you behind
      me on *Beaumonde,*
And off we shall trot on a jaunt to Loch
    Lomond.

          Your devoted and faithful admirer.

DULL NESS CASTLE, 1821.

LETTER TO MRS. GILLIES.

A THOUGHT has this minute come into my head,
That all my good friends must be thinking
    I 'm dead,
For since Jean went abroad, which is six
    months and more,
The shade of a Whig has not darkened my door;
And it 's no sae lang syne nor diffiquilt to mind,
At bridals- and bur'als and a' ploys of the kind,
So great was the kindness we had for each
    ither,
Pitlyal and the Gillies aye herded thegither.
So you and Lord Gillies might baith ha'e kent
    better
Than heed such a tale unconfirmed by a letter.
But I 've found out the nest where the rumour
    was hatched,
And how it took wing with a swiftness un-
    matched ;
How it flew all abroad like some magical spell,
And how puir Jean was telt it at Aix-la-
    Chapelle.

Letter to Mrs.
Gillies from
the Lady
Pitlyal.
1821.

Your cousin, Miss Clem, is an arrant de-
ceiver,

A marvel to me any one should believe her;

And Mistress George Russell had better be-
ware

Lest her wit, running wild, lead her into a
snare;

For the joke either argues a great want of sense,

Or impeaches the schemers of *malice pre-
pense*—

A plot I'm determined they both shall rue
dearly,

And, cost what it will, shall be punished
severely.

While one spark of justice remains in our laws,

My well-beloved Jeffrey shall plead in my
cause,

And William Clerk, also, will make them
hear reason,

Though he gaed by my door in Angus this
season;

But the Rosebud was absent, and nae doubt
that he

Thought a call might gi'e fash to an auld wife
like me.

Our prophecie treats more than once of a tryal,

And the fame of a law-loving Lady Pitlyal;

F

Then in sentences dark appears whiles to
    foretell
Of an action she raised in revenge on hersel'.

Jean calls this " the prophet's prophetical
    fiction,"
To me it appears a mysterious prediction,
Expounding, as *I* do, " The triumph and fame"
To Pitlyal, will yet be fulfilled in her name.

She's a fine creature Jean, and has as
    mickle sense
As mony young misses wi' twice her pretence;
And yet at your parties she said she felt shy,
When a person addressed her, to give a reply;
For she wanted the courage to speak conver-
    sation,
And hold up like other young folk of her
    station.
Though I spared not my siller to have her
    braw dressed,
And she lookit, I thought, as genteel as the
    rest,
She would laugh and declare 't was the dress-
    maker's garnish,
The manner was wanting, the polish, the
    varnish;

And casting a look on her gossamer frock,
Said she 'minded hersel' of a milliner's block.

What think you I've done?—after pondering fairly,
I've sent her abroad to her cousins of Airlie;
She has seen Waterloo, she has sailed on the Rhine,
And she's been to the place where they mak' the Hock wine;
She rested some time baith at Basle and Lucerne,
And she spent fifteen weeks in the Canton of Berne;
She's now got to Paris, and winter once over,
I plan setting forward to meet her at Dover.

Now believe me, with every good wish and kind word
To my Whig friends, including yourself and your lord,
He'll mind how I told him the last time I saw him,
We'd planted *East Ireland** and ploughed *Capernaum.**

  * The names of two grass fields on Pitlyal.

Letter to Mrs.
Gillies from
the Lady
Pitlyal.
1821.

'T was in this very plantin', close by the
    mill-lade,
That I foolishly dreamt I had angered Holm-
    head.
And now fare ye weel, and remember me by
    all
The auld-warld havers of Lady Pitlyal.

THE BIRKIE O' BONNIE DUNDEE.

YE fair lands of Angus and bonnie Dundee,
How dear are your echoes, your memories
    to me!
At gatherings and meetings in a' the braw
    toons,
I danced wi' the lasses and distanced the
    loons;
Syne bantered them gaily, and bade the young
    men
Be mair on their mettle when I cam' again.
They jeered me, they cheered me, and cried
    ane and a',
He's no an ill fellow that, now he's awa.

When puir beggar bodies cam' making their
    mane,
I spak them aye cheery, for siller I'd nane,
They shook up their duddies, and muttered,
    "Wae's me,
"Sae lightsome a laddie no worth a bawbee!"

I played wi' the bairnies at bowls and at ba',
And left them a' greeting when I cam' awa;
Aye! mithers, and bairnies, and lassies and a',
Were a' sobbin' loudly when I cam' awa.

I feigned a gay laugh, just to keep in the greet,
For ae bonnie lassie, sae douce and sae sweet,
How matchless the blink of her deep loving
    e'e,
How soft fell its shade as it glanced upon me.
I flung her a wild rose sae fresh and sae fair,
And bade it bloom on in the bright summer
    there;
While breathing its fragrance, she aiblins may
    gi'e
A thought to the Birkie o' bonnie Dundee.

WORTHIES.

THERE were some worthies connected with Duntrune, whose names must not be forgot in these reminiscences. They were not "children of the mist," but pure, sterling characters, the first and most perfect of whom was Meg Matthew, whose habitation was opposite to my grandfather Mr. Graham's house, in Arbroath, and who lived on familiar terms with the family.

Worthies.

MEG MATTHEW.

Looking through the long vista of the present century, and far down into the past, I see myself, a little girl of five or six years old, sitting on a *creepy*[1] at the feet of a remarkable old woman called Meg Matthew.

Meg Matthew.

Meg sat at her wheel spinning flax

[1] A stool.

with both hands from the waist, while I gazed on her dear, homely, wrinkled face, drinking in the old-world tales of her past life; her dress, a short-gown, woollen petticoat, a striped wincey apron, a close white mutch with a black hood over it.

She had been a servant in the family of the minister of St. Vigeans. The minister and his wife both died during her service, leaving three children, two boys and a girl, totally unprovided for. Upon which Meg engaged an attic room in the Market-gate of Arbroath, and carried the orphans there with her, where she span to maintain them, and she begged or extorted from those she thought could afford it, their schooling and clothing.

She did not ask like a mendicant, but said she *must have* such and such things for her bairns; and when the boys were to be fitted out, she would call at various places, tell the lady that she must have linen, and that the young ladies must set to wark and make so many shirts for Jamie or Willy.

Situations were procured for the boys;

one settled in the West Indies, the other in Montreal, and after the lapse of years, Willy returned in good circumstances, and died in Arbroath. James married in Montreal, became affluent, and sent his daughter home to visit her aunt, and the friends who had known Meg. She was an accomplished lady-like young person.

Meg went herself to London with the boys, to see them fitted out, and witness their departure; and she saw King George the Third, whom she described as being "like ony ither husbandman wi' a stand o' blue claes."

Betsy obtained a lady's-maid's place in Hopetoun House, where she remained till her marriage with Mr. Haldane, a stocking manufacturer in Haddington. He left her a widow in comfort; she was much respected, and died in a good old age.

Meg was the theme of many conversations among the young ladies of Hopetoun and their attendant; her name and fame were even well known among the servants.

One day a housemaid ran into the

room calling out, "Miss Cruickshank, if your Meg be in the body, she is now coming up the road, dressed in her Sabbath-day claes, and her plaid ower her head."[1]

It was Meg herself, arrived on foot from Arbroath, and rapturously she was welcomed by the whole family. She would remain only a few days, declining all favours for herself ; and when they offered to show her through the house, replied, "Na, na ; I'm no gaen to big the marrow of it."

She returned home to her spinning-wheel in her solitary little room ; and from her rather unsocial manners, she was looked upon by coarse-minded people in the light of a witch, or one who was in compact with the devil.

I remember her last illness, and seeing her laid in her coffin.

Her dust rests within the cemetery of the old Abbey of Arbroath,

Embalmed in memory with things that are holy.

---

[1] Mr. Cruickshank was minister of St. Vigeans, near Arbroath.

JOHN FRASER,

A waggish old man who served the family John Fraser. at Duntrune a term of sixty years, and during three generations of its owners. He was cook there when I was about ten years of age.

He was not the type of a *chef-de-cuisine* of the present day, but a very excellent cook in his way. He dressed in a dark waistcoat, knee-breeches, and a red night-cap.

He liked no *helper* in the kitchen, and always sent out any of the other servants who invaded his domain, shriek-ing with laughter.

He preferred his beer to his meat, and never partook of meals with his fellows, but sat behind and joked with them at dinner.

He was very kind to my sister and me, and when he had no other dainty to bestow, he would boil a fresh egg, or parch peas for us; and sometimes he contrived to make us a whistle of what he called a *guse-thrapple* (*Anglicè*, the windpipe of a goose).

In the years 1745 and 1746, when his master, my grandfather, was skulking after the battle of Culloden, John found it imperative to take other service, and hired himself to Mr. Wedderburn of Pearsie; but he wearied to get back to Duntrune.

One day Mr. Wedderburn observed him putting a spit through a peat, probably with the intention of cleaning it. When his master inquired his reason for so doing, he replied, "Indeed, sir, I'm just gaen to roast a peat, for fear I forget my trade."

At the end of two years he returned to Duntrune, where he continued to exercise his calling during the remainder of his life. His death took place in Dundee, where his master, my uncle, paid the last tribute of respect to his memory, and laid his head in the grave beside the family he had served so faithfully. John's widow was so gratified with the respect paid to her husband, that she called her neighbours to "come oot and see the *beautiful burial.*"

There is an anecdote of John worthy of remembrance. One day he sent up a roast goose for dinner, off which he, or some one, had cut a leg before it appeared on the table. John was summoned from the kitchen to tell how the goose came to be deprived of a leg; to which he replied, that all the geese of Duntrune had only one leg, and in corroboration of this assertion, he pointed to a whole flock in front of the house, which were happily sitting asleep on one leg, with a sentinel on the watch.

The Laird opened the window, clapped his hands, and cried "*whew*," on which they all got up on two legs and took wing. But John, no way discomfited, quietly told his master, "If ye had clappit your hands and cried *whew* to the ane on the table, it would maist likely ha'e dune the same."

It is not to be believed that John ever read Boccaccio, or had ever heard of the Venetian cook "*Chichibio*," who played the same trick with the crane's leg; but it is possible that two artists in the same vocation, even with four centuries rolling between them, may have originated similar ideas.

David Murray,

Whom I never saw, served at the same time in the capacity of butler.

When asked what became of the wine that was left, he replied, "I boot ha'e the bottles to wash."

The Cadger.

An old cadger who brought fish to Duntrune, used to sit sound asleep on the cart, leaving the fish to the discretion of his horse.

One day he arrived at the door nearly frozen to death, and was carried into the kitchen to be thawed. In due time they gave him some food, and a glass of warm toddy to drink, which so cheered his heart, that he exclaimed, "Oh! sirs, I am happy wi' ye; I am just ae *eild* wi' the auld King George III., and I daur say I am as happy a man as he is. The leddy will be takin' a glass o' this till hersel' when she comes in frae her walk; for I am sure naebody could ha'e it in the hoose and no tak' it."

THE BEGGAR.

An old woman was a frequent visitor at Duntrune. She was called *Bobbins*, a nickname she did not particularly like, in consequence of some delinquency on her part.

My aunt, Miss Alison Grahame, very many years her junior, gave her a full suit of winter clothing, in reply to which she exclaimed, " Gudeness! woman, what will I do when ye dee ?"

In spite of the warm clothing, however, she was seized with a severe cold, and confined to bed, and the neighbours sent donations of various delicacies, one of which was a jar of black currant jam, which she desired might be *"toomed"* into a large wooden dish, and she sat up in bed to eat it with a horn spoon, making wry faces all the time, and took credit to herself for the same, by remarking, that " mony ane wouldna sup it, for the lady makes her jeil wi' the *caff*[1] amang 't."

[1] Chaff.

After this repast she drank six bottles of beer, half a bottle of whisky, and fell sound asleep for eight-and-forty hours; at the end of which time she awoke quite recovered.

THE DOGS.

We had a Skye terrier named Oscar, which had a particular affection for Nanny the dairymaid, and always accompanied her to the milking of the cows, for which attention she rewarded him with a basin of warm milk. He always went with her to her father's house at Linlathen on the Sunday evenings, a distance of two miles, after having been to the Established Church at Murroes; but on occasion of the opening of the Free Church in the parish of Monifieth, which is not far from the dwelling of Nanny's parents, he went there alone, remained in the tent during the forenoon service, was observed among the congregation in the new building in the afternoon, and we supposed he must have remained to the evening service, as he did not appear at home till past eleven o'clock at night, when he gave tongue at the window of Nanny's room.

Once or twice after this Nanny had inadvertently gone from home without him, and he had observed her caressing some strange dogs on the road, which threw him into such a paroxysm of jealousy that he nearly demolished her wardrobe. He went to the room where she and the other maid-servants kept their clothes, drew two of her best caps from a basket, carried them down-stairs and hid them among some shavings in the stick-house; being unable to extract the straw-bonnet from the basket, he chewed the strings of it, and tore up a handkerchief, and finished off by selecting a printed gown of hers from among those of her fellow-servants, and tore it to shreds.

Great was poor Nanny's consternation when she discovered that the creature who she always said " had mair wit than mony bodies," should be guilty of such misconduct, so she gave him a good thrashing, and he vanished from the house. No one saw him again for a couple of days, Nanny looking very mysterious all the time, and feeling assured that he had "ower muckle wut."

The first intimation I received of his delinquency was from himself, when he came crouching to my feet, and looking up into my face, as if entreating forgiveness.

He did not go to the byre with Nanny for more than a week after this; but, on mature deliberation, he made an advance to lick her hands, and she restored him to favour.

Oscar lived to a good old age, and died a natural death.

There was a general wish that another native of Skye should be got to supply his place. We had not far to look for a successor, as there was a handsome fellow at Pitkerrow judged worthy; one, too, which had a peculiarly knowing look, from an accidental drooping of one ear, while the other remained erect; he had also a custom of running on three legs, while he carried the fourth like a bird on the wing.

A contract was agreed on, and Birkie seemed satisfied with the transfer, the distance being within a mile from his early home with the miller, to which he could easily run down to see how his friends there got on without him, for he was a creature of kindly affections, and kept up an interest in the bairns, with whom he had many merry gambols, and over whom he kept a faithful watch when father and mother were absent from the house.

At Duntrune he found many domestic affairs to look after, especially that of attending on Meggy Scott while she made the porridge in the morning for dogs and cats, and being of a liberal disposition, she gave them abundance of milk and other good things.

After breakfast he followed Meggy to the garden to see her gather fruit and flowers, then he would lie down under the elm tree at the kitchen gate, where he could hear every footstep, and see every person who approached the house, giving warning either by a growl, a snappish bark, or a note of welcome to let the servants understand the quality of the visitors. He had a high opinion of his own prowess; when a carriage moved from the door he would run between the wheels, at the risk of his life, giving tongue with all the strength of his lungs, in the belief that it was his force that gave the impetus.

When any of the household made him jealous by fondling the big dog Neptune, he would run off to the miller's, and remain for days, sometimes for weeks, till a friend went to bring him home, and then he returned in the full confidence of a welcome greeting.

In the course of time he became rheumatic, and though able for the walk down to Pitkerrow, he felt rather stiff and incapable of mounting the hill again, and would lie at the miller's door till the carriage should pass that way, rejoicing to be picked up, and drive home on the box.

The last time he attempted to climb the brae, a mischievous boy, who was sent out to scare the crows, fired a gun at him, and he never ventured beyond the gate again.

I have said he was a creature of kindly affections, but he was also *a wylie, and a pridefu' doggie;* indeed, he carried his crest so high when walking in the company of ladies, that he did not even acknowledge the miller on the road.

Once, too, when the worthy man came to Duntrune with a sack of meal, he turned tail and would not see him, for which misconduct, when reproached for his ingratitude, he flashed a supercilious glance on his monitors, and walked off.

Poor dear Birkie has now passed away, and been lamented.

Another descendant of a Skye family, and rejoicing in the name of Jack, rules in his stead. He is of a gentler nature, with black muzzle and a coat of fine long yellow hair that touches the ground, and waves round him like a gleam of light as he bounds along the terrace.

Some one may perhaps write his life when his days come to an end.

JOHN AND FANNY FRASER.

AMONG the worthies and kinsfolk who paid an annual visit at Duntrune, were an elderly brother and sister—Mr. John and Miss Fanny Fraser.

Descended from, and allied to, many of the gentry in the county of Angus, they always met a cordial welcome among friends and relatives, thus keeping up their respectable status in society.

In the first edition of this volume, in consequence of a misapprehension, it is stated that Mr. Fraser had retired from the Navy with a pension of forty pounds a year;—such was not the case; but his old age was made independent by the bounty of his cousin, Major Fraser of Hospitalfield, near Arbroath, one of the most genial and generous of men, to whose memory this statement is due.

The brother and sister resided in their paternal property—*an old house in St. Andrews.*

They were of a rare simplicity of character, and so devoted to each other, there seemed to be but one mind between them ; whatever suggestion or remark was uttered by the one was echoed by the other.

Steadfast in their faith, loving God with all their soul, their neighbour as themselves, they held out a helping hand to the lowly wherever they felt there was power in it to be of use ; in proof of which they adopted the child of a black woman who came from the East in attendance on a family, and in whose service she desired to remain, while her child could not be admitted as an appendage. Our friends received the little Hindu girl, delighting in her simple language, repeating and re-echoing her quaint sayings, her marvellous wisdom ! ! !

In the course of a few years their little fondling sickened and died, a dispensation that nearly broke the hearts of her bene-factors ; indeed, they were inconsolable and deaf to all moral comfort, when a happy thought struck the grateful mother of the departed one, that another black child might bring them consolation, and she spared neither time nor trouble in the

search till she found one, though of a
darker race, and presented it to the sor-
rowing pair. Poor Mr. and Miss Fraser
were overwhelmed with perplexity; but
when the dear little woolly-head looked
up to them so confidingly, nestling itself in their bosoms and their affections,
they accepted the gift as a blessing from
Heaven, gave it their name and their
home, and were comforted.

Some months after the adoption of the
second Betsy, John succeeded to a small
villa on the south side of Edinburgh by
the death of his aunt, Lady Wood of
Bonnington, and they removed to this
new home after disposing of all their
interests in St. Andrews.

Betsy Fraser grew up to repay them
with the tenderest affection, loving and
dutiful as a daughter, nursing them in
sickness, watching over them at the hour
of death.

They bequeathed to her the villa, which
was all their worldly wealth.

She married a most respectable man,
and they live in one of the pretty fishing

towns on the east coast of Fife, where he carries on a lucrative business connected with the sea. They are surrounded by an interesting family, and they still retain possession of Fraser Lodge.

MISS MENIE TROTTER.

In Lord Cockburn's *Memorials of his Time*, he speaks of " a singular race of excellent old Scotch ladies. They were a delightful set; strong-headed, warm-hearted, and high-spirited; the fire of their tempers not always latent; merry, even in solitude; very resolute; indifferent about the modes and habits of the modern world; and adhering to their own ways, so as to stand out, like primitive rocks, above ordinary society. Their prominent qualities of sense, humour, affection, and spirit, were embodied in curious outsides; for they all dressed, and spoke, and did exactly as they chose; their language, like their habits, entirely Scotch, but without any other vulgarity than what perfect naturalness is sometimes mistaken for."

At page 65 there is notice of Miss Menie Trotter of the Mortonhall family ; but he gives only the outer shell of the character, such as he remembered her in his boyhood, little aware of the well of deep feeling that lay hid within that rough piece of granite; how it would spring up at odd times, and flow freely in some eccentric channel, sending fresh soil to the youthful plant, carrying substance to the needy, and comfort to the weary heart.[1]

[1] "Miss Menie Trotter, of the Mortonhall family, was of a later date. She was of the agrestic order. Her pleasures lay in the fields and long country walks. Ten miles at a stretch, within a few years of her death, was nothing to her. Her attire accorded. But her understanding was fully as masculine. Though slenderly endowed, she did, unnoticed, acts of liberality for which most of the rich would expect to be advertised. Prevailing loneliness gave her some entertaining habits, but never impaired her enjoyment of her friends, for whom she had always diverting talk, and occasionally 'a bit denner.' Indeed, she generally sacrificed an ox to hospitality every autumn, which, according to a system of her own, she ate regularly from nose to tail ; and as she indulged in him only on Sundays, and with a chosen few, he feasted her half through the winter. This was at Blackford Cottage, a melancholy villa on the north side of Blackford Hill, where the last half, at the least, of her life was passed. I remember her urging her neighbour, Sir Thomas Lauder,

She was penurious in small things, but her generosity could rise to circumstances. Her dower was an annuity from the estate of Mortonhall. She had a contempt for securities, and would trust no bank with her money, but kept all her bills and bank-notes in a green silk bag that hung on her toilette glass. On each side of the table stood a large white bowl, one of

not long before her death, to dine with her next Sunday—'For eh! Sir Thammas! we 're terrible near the tail noo.' She told me that her oldest friends were the Inneses of Stow and the Scotts of Malleny— families she had known for above eighty-five years. They and the Mortonhall family had each a mansion-house in town; two of them being the two corner houses at the lower end of a close leading from the High Street down to the Cowgate, and the third one of the corner houses opposite, at the lower end of the close leading from the Cowgate southwards; each of the three houses looking into both the Cowgate and the close. The Cowgate has now lost half its character by getting a large sewer under ground; but before this innovation 'the Coogate Strand,' as it was called, when in flood, was a great torrent, not filling the cellars merely, but almost the whole canal of the street. I remember a station on its banks, near Holy-rood, where there was a regular net fishery, to catch what the stream brought down, particularly corks. Miss Trotter described the delight of the children of these families in wading in that gutter when it was safe."

which contained her silver, the other her copper money, the latter always full to the brim, accessible to Peggy, her hand-maid, or any other servant in the house, for the idea of any one stealing money never entered her brain. Indeed, she once sent a present to her niece, Mrs. Cun-inghame, of a fifty-pound note wrapped up in a cabbage-leaf, and intrusted it to the care of a woman who was going with a basket of butter to the Edinburgh market. My friend Mrs. Cuninghame related to me this and the following his-tories of her aunt :—

One day, in the course of conversation, she said to her niece, "Do ye ken, Mar-garet, that Mrs. Thomas R—— is dead. I was gaun by the door this morning, and thought I would just look in and speer for her. She was very near her end, but quite sensible, and expressed her gratitude to God for what He had done for her and her fatherless bairns. She said 'She was leaving a large young family with very small means, but she had that trust in *Him* that they would not be forsaken, and that He would provide for them.' Now, Margaret, ye'll tell Peggy to bring down the green silk bag that hangs on the corner of my looking-glass, and ye'll tak' twa thousand pounds out o' it, and gi'e it to Walter Ferrier for behoof of thae orphan bairns; it will fit out the laddies, and be something to the lassies. I want to make good the words, 'that God wad provide for them,' for what else was I sent that way this morning, but as a humble instrument in His hands?" Miss Trotter had a friendship for a certain Mrs. B——, who had an only son, and he was looked on as a simpleton, but his relatives had interest to get him a situation as clerk in a bank, where he contrived to steal money to the extent of five hundred pounds. His peculations were discovered, and in those days he would have been hanged, but Miss Trotter hearing the report started instantly for Edinburgh, went to the bank, and ascertained the truth. She at once laid down five hundred pounds, telling them, "Ye maun not only stop proceedings, but ye maun keep him in the bank in some capacity, however mean, till I find some other employment for him." Then she fitted the lad out, and sent him to London, .where she had a friend to whom she wrote, offering another five hundred pounds to any one who would procure him a situation abroad, in which he might gain an honest living, and never be trusted with money.

After all this was settled, she went herself and communicated the facts to his mother.

When she was confined to bed, and felt that her end was approaching, she bid Mrs. Cuninghame look at a little coarse engraving of a young man that hung on the wall of her room in a black frame.

"Do ye ken, Margaret, whase picture that is? I would like to tell you about it. That's Jamie Pitcairn; he was but a young medical student in thae days, but he rose to distinction in his profession after that.

"He was of a noble nature, and had a kindly heart, and he was the only one in the whole world that ever showed me any tenderness or affection; and weel did I love him; indeed, we were deeply attached to ane anither.

"My mother and my sister Johanna were proud and overbearing, and looked down upon Jamie, but my auldest sister, Mrs. Douglas, had a mair feeling heart, and often took me with her to visit at Dr. Cullen's,[1] where I met Jamie, and mony

[1] A pleasant glimpse of Dr. Cullen's fireside may be obtained by referring to the travels of M. Faujas Saint-Fond, who visited Edinburgh in the year 1784. He says, "Dr. Cullen lived in the midst of a numerous family, who formed around him an amiable circle of friends. Good-nature and amenity reigned in his house. This learned physician merited all these advantages, for he himself possessed manners and a disposition of the most agreeable kind. I found that he very much resembled Buffon in his behaviour and mode of living, which rendered him doubly interesting to me. His table was plentifully served, but without any luxury. I was, however, astonished to find a profusion of punch brought in between the dessert and tea. This regimen in the house of a physician of such great reputation appeared to me very extraordinary. He observed my surprise, and said to me with a smile, that this beverage was not only suited to his age, but that a long experience had convinced him that when taken with moderation it was very salutary for the inhabitants of Scotland, particularly during the latter part of the autumnal season, and in winter, because

happy hours we spent there. Whiles he wad come and drink tea with Mrs. Douglas; her house was at the head of the Links, and the windows looked out upon the country and up to Arthur's Seat and the Salisbury Craigs. One evening we three sat there building our airy castles; a happy party; the beautiful warld before us, and the birds singing joyously, when the door opened, and four black eyes like a thunder-cloud darkened the room. They fell upon me like a spell that froze my very heart's blood. I can never forget the look of disdain they coost upon Jamie. He never spoke, but took up his hat, gave one kind look to me,

the cold humidity which then prevails in this climate often checks perspiring. *Punch*, he remarked, *is a warm stimulant which operates wonderfully in maintaining that necessary secretion, or in restoring it to its equilibrium.*"

M. Faujas Saint-Fond adds naïvely, "This humid and penetrating atmosphere had for some time affected me in a very disagreeable manner, notwithstanding the active life which I led. . . . This disagreeable feeling was not to be endured, and I resolved to adopt the regimen of Dr. Cullen. Each day after dinner I took a glass of punch, which soon restored me to my usual condition."

opened the door and left the room, and I never saw him again.

"They were cruel to me. I was ta'en hame to suffer, and he never married.

"I had no friend left, for Mrs. Douglas went to France for the education of her only daughter, who in course of time became Lady Dick of Prestonfield. So I wandered among the hills, and held communion with Him who is the father of the afflicted, and when I looked over the varied land and the restless sea, and down upon the broom and the flowers that were offering up their mute praise and incense to their Creator, I found 'the comfort that passes understanding.'

"Mony ane thought when I gaed thae long walks among the mountains, that I was my lane; but I never was my lane, for the Maker of this beautiful world was my constant companion."

She was a great reader, and had a highly-cultivated mind; but, continuing her remarks, said: "I never cared muckle for religious books; indeed, the only twa books that I thought worth reading were

Massillon's Sermons and the New Testament. I didna gae often to the kirk, for I never profited by their lang prayers and their weary sermons; and I had nae pleasure in looking at the braw folk that cam' there on the Sundays."

Pointing again to the engraving, she added, "Now, that's the picture of Jamie Pitcairn." A day or two after this conversation, Mrs. Cuninghame paid her another visit, and found her still in life, but very feeble; on asking how she felt, she replied, "Very weel, but the candle is just done."

She fell asleep the same evening, and her soul returned to Him who gave it.

WHITE IS THE SNOWFLAKE.

Oh ! white is the snowflake that falls on the
mountain,
  Ere the breath of this world hath sullied
  its pride,
And clear is the wave where it breaks from
the fountain,
  Ere the touch of the earth hath polluted its
  tide,
    And fair was existence ere sin threw a
    blight,
    For the Spirit came pure from the Author
    of Light.

Lo ! the fairest of flowers shall be nipped in
their bloom,
  All their beauty and loveliness strewed
  on the ground,
And the dearest of ties shall be hid by the
tomb,
  While the mildew of death sheds its poison
  around.

But the " Day-spring on High " beams
   bright o'er the grave,
For the *Word* of Jehovah is mighty to
   save.

He hath trampled on death, He hath con-
   quered the foe,
  All the strongholds of darkness asunder are
   riven ;
He hath laid all the hosts of the enemy low,
  And restored to mankind the lost image of
   Heaven.
    He is gone to prepare for the faithful a
    place,
    And the Comforter's sent to the whole
    human race.

Finis.

EDINBURGH : T. CONSTABLE,
PRINTER TO THE QUEEN, AND TO THE UNIVERSITY.

www.ingramcontent.com/pod-product-compliance
Lightning Source LLC
Chambersburg PA
CBHW020750020726
47495CB00008B/2361